# Dunc and the Haunted Castle

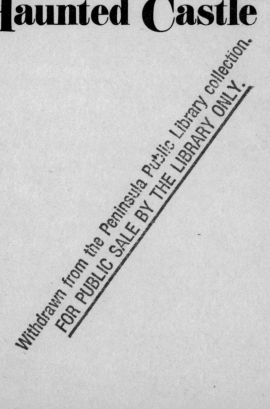

YEARLING BOOKS/YOUNG YEARLINGS/YEARLING CLASSICS are designed especially to entertain and enlighten young people. Patricia Reilly Giff, consultant to this series, received her bachelor's degree from Marymount College and a master's degree in history from St. John's University. She holds a Professional Diploma in Reading and a Doctorate of Humane Letters from Hofstra University. She was a teacher and reading consultant for many years and is the author of numerous books for young readers.

For a complete listing of all Yearling titles,
write to Dell Readers Service,
P.O. Box 1045, South Holland, IL 60473.

# Gary Paulsen

# Dunc and the Haunted Castle

**A YEARLING BOOK**

*243 1378*

Published by
Dell Publishing
a division of
Bantam Doubleday Dell Publishing Group, Inc.
1540 Broadway
New York, New York 10036

ISBN: 0-440-40893-8

Printed in the United States of America

December 1993

10  9  8  7  6  5  4  3  2  1

OPM

# Dunc and the Haunted Castle

# **Chapter · 1**

Amos Binder was in his room reading a letter from his cousin, T.J. Tyler.

. . . so my dad rented this really old castle for the summer. He has some research to do here in Scotland and he brought me with him. That's where you guys come in. He doesn't have much time to spend with me so he says he'd be glad to fly you over to keep me company. What do you say?

Sincerely, T.J.

P.S. Weird things are going on around here. I could use some help.

1

"What do you make of that?" Amos handed the letter to Duncan—Dunc—Culpepper, his best friend for life.

Dunc studied the letter. "That last part's kind of mysterious. Sounds like he needs us."

"Yeah, that's what I thought too. I guess I'd be willing to give up my date with Melissa to go to Scotland."

"Amos, you don't have a date with Melissa."

Melissa Hansen was the light of Amos's life. As far as Amos was concerned, no other girl compared to her. Melissa gave Amos about as much thought as she gave an ant crawling on the sidewalk. Actually, she'd probably give more thought to the ant.

"Not officially," Amos said. "But she tried to call last night to ask me to the youth club dance."

"What do you mean, she *tried* to call?"

"The phone rang while I was in my room composing a letter to Dear Abby about the incredible injustice of a person being grounded for the rest of his life just because of a small accident involving their dad's power saw and the garage door."

"Wait a minute," Dunc said. "You never told me you were grounded!"

Amos shrugged. "It didn't last long because after the phone call I'm no longer grounded. Now I'm up for adoption."

"What did you destroy this time?"

"Nothing. For once, I didn't ruin anything."

"Your parents want to farm you out, and you didn't mess anything up? Are you sure?"

Amos nodded. "It was like this. When the phone rang, I knew it was Melissa. Her ring has that rare three beats to a pulse."

Amos claimed he could tell Melissa's ring from anybody else's. Dunc knew it was impossible, not only because his research indicated that Amos's phone rang the same way every time but because Melissa Hansen wouldn't call someone who didn't rate any higher than an ant.

"Anyway," Amos continued, "I had to get it on that all-important first ring. So I headed for the nearest phone."

"Which was in?"

"My sister's room. She just got one installed for her birthday."

"So far it doesn't sound so awful."

3

Amos slapped his knee. "That's what I said. Too bad my sister and the other cheerleaders didn't see it that way."

"Cheerleaders?"

"Yeah. How was I supposed to know they were all in there trying on new uniforms?"

Dunc raised one eyebrow.

"I really didn't see a thing. Honest. You know how I am when it comes to the telephone. Pure concentration."

"Right. Did you get to the phone?"

"Yes and no. Things sort of went crazy in there. Girls were running everywhere. Amy was yelling names at me that I can't repeat. And the rest of them started throwing things. Have you ever been hit full in the face with an electric hair dryer?"

Dunc shook his head and tried not to smile. "No, I can't say I have."

"I was knocked out cold. When I came to, I had the telephone wrapped around my head and two pom-poms stuck up my nose. One in each nostril. I barely escaped with my life. And of course Amy made it sound to my parents like I was the original peeping Tom or something. Needless to say, my folks think my going to Scotland is a wonderful idea."

4

Dunc turned his attention back to the letter. "Does T.J. still quote his Ethiopian grandmother?"

Amos nodded. "In his last letter he wrote 'The moon is only small if you sit on a duck.' I'm still trying to figure that one out."

Dunc smiled. "T.J.'s a character. Has he invented anything new since we saw him last?"

"The last I heard, he was working on flying shoes. He built some kind of device into his shoes that lifts him off the ground when he walks. It still has a few bugs, though. When his feet come up, his face comes down. Usually into the pavement."

"Sounds like our buddy T.J.," Dunc said.

# Chapter·2

"Look for a tall African-American man and a kid wearing a trench coat," Amos said.

"I'm looking." Dunc carefully observed each person in the steady stream of people walking back and forth in the crowded Scottish airport. "I don't see them."

"They should be here. T.J. said he and his dad would pick us up."

"They probably had a flat tire or something." Dunc stopped. "You did send the telegram telling them which plane we were on and what time it landed, didn't you?"

Amos looked offended. "Give me a little credit here."

"Okay. It's just that sometimes, in the

past, you have been known to screw things up."

"Well, not this time. I distinctly remember putting the message in my pocket and riding my bike downtown, and—" Amos hesitated.

"What?"

"I just thought of something. On my way to send the message I ran into Dennis Therman. You remember Dennis? The kids at school used to call him Lizard Lips."

"I remember him. What does he have to do with the telegram?"

"Dennis said he was only going to be in town for a few days. So we decided to go to the arcade for a while."

"You didn't send it."

"Well, actually, I—"

"You didn't send it."

Amos shook his head.

Dunc sat on his suitcase. "Here we are in the largest airport in Scotland. It's nearly dark. We don't know a soul, and we're not being met by anyone. Tell me you at least have T.J.'s phone number."

Amos chewed on a fingernail and looked at the ceiling.

**8**

Dunc closed his eyes. "Never mind. You don't have to tell me."

"They're over here, Dad!" T.J. ran up to them out of breath. "We were afraid we missed you guys."

"T.J." Amos grinned. "Am I glad to see you."

Dunc knew better than to try to shake T.J.'s hand. The last time he tried it, an alarm in T.J.'s trench coat had gone off and red lights started flashing. "That goes double for me, T.J. But how did you know we were here?"

"There's this creepy old lady who keeps house for us. She reads the future in tea leaves, and she told us we'd be having visitors today."

T.J.'s dad walked up. "But that's not how we knew you'd be here. Amos's mother found a message in his shirt pocket. She thought she'd better double-check and make sure we knew when you were coming. She called us last night."

"But there really is this witch"—T.J.'s dad threw him a look—"I mean, this lady, who reads tea leaves and does all kinds of spooky things. Wait till you meet her."

9

# Chapter · 3

T.J.'s dad put the suitcases in the back of the rented station wagon. "As soon as I get a chance, I'm going to trade this wagon in for a four-wheel drive. The road leading up to the castle is a little rough."

"The realtor, Mr. Macbeth, told us that's the reason we got the castle so cheap," T.J. said. "Normally castles, even small ones like ours, aren't for rent, and when they are, nobody can afford them."

Amos hit his head on the roof of the car. He jerked his seat belt tighter. "How much farther?"

"We're almost there." T.J. pointed out the

window. "Dunbar Castle is just on the other side of that hill."

"Is that the owner's name?" Dunc asked.

T.J. shrugged. "We've never met the owner. Mr. Macbeth said the owner is a recluse and wants to remain anonymous. Dad sends the rent checks to the realtor."

Dunc rubbed his chin. "That's strange. I wonder why. . . ."

"Don't look a gift castle in the mouth," Amos said. "Especially one with servants."

Mr. Tyler glanced back at Amos. "There are only two people who work full time at the castle. Mrs. Knox and Mr. Smith. Sometimes Mrs. Knox's son Jimmy works part time. The owner hired them more to keep the place in good condition than to wait on us."

"Mrs. Knox is the one I told you about," T.J. whispered. "The witch."

Mr. Tyler frowned. "Mrs. Knox isn't a witch. She's just a little odd. Some of the old Scottish traditions are different from what you're used to."

"Who's Mr. Smith?" Dunc asked.

"The grounds keeper. He's strange too," T.J. said. "He's always watching me. Everywhere I go, he's there. He sort of pops up out of nowhere."

T.J.'s dad drove across a bridge and through a large open iron gate. "Here we are, boys. Dunbar Castle."

The courtyard was dimly lit. A tall, thin man with a red beard appeared from the shadows and started unloading the suitcases.

"Boys, this is Mr. Smith." T.J.'s dad took one of the suitcases. "Mr. Smith, this is Amos Binder and Duncan Culpepper."

Mr. Smith stared at Dunc. "Duncan. Now that's a fine Scottish name." He turned away abruptly and carried the boys' things through the massive oak front door.

Amos looked at T.J. "Are all the natives as friendly as he is?"

"I told you he was strange." T.J. led them inside the dark castle. "This big room is what they call the great hall."

"I'd probably be impressed—if I could see it," Amos said. "Don't people in Scotland believe in electricity?"

Mr. Tyler handed Amos a candle. "That's one of the problems with being so far out. We're on a generator. The place is too big for the generator to light up everything all at once, so at night we use candles." He gave a candle to T.J. "Show the boys their rooms. I'll see if Mrs. Knox left us anything for supper."

T.J. headed for the stairs. "Follow me."

The flickering light of Amos's candle cast eerie shadows on the wall as they climbed the stone staircase. "This place is kind of spooky."

"Mrs. Knox told me the place is haunted." T.J. stopped in front of a suit of armor. "By the guy who used to wear this. Robert Ramsey. There's a full-length painting of him down in the library."

"Who is he?" Dunc asked.

"Mr. Knox says he's a hero. There was a big battle fought not too far from here, and this Ramsey guy gave his life defending the Stone of Scone, the Scottish symbol of royal authority."

Dunc took a closer look at the armor. "What makes her think he haunts the castle?"

"She says he was beheaded during the battle and at night he walks the ramparts looking for his head."

Amos shivered. "You left out the part about a headless ghost in your letter."

"Is this ghost business what you needed our help with?" Dunc asked.

"Keep your voice down," T.J. whispered. "You never know who might be listening. Come on. I'll show you where your rooms are. We'll talk about it after supper."

A gust of wind came out of nowhere. T.J.'s candle blew out. Someone grabbed Dunc from behind and pulled him into a secret passage in the wall.

Amos held his candle up. He took a couple of faltering steps. "T.J.? Dunc? Where are you guys?"

The row of paintings hanging on the wall seemed to be glaring down at him. There was something about one of them. He brought his candle closer.

The eyes in the painting moved.

# Chapter · 4

Amos was still mad. "It wasn't funny. I nearly messed my pants."

"I'm sorry, Amos," T.J. said. "I was just trying to prove my point."

"What was your point?" Amos sneered. "To see how long it would take me to have a major heart attack?"

"I said I was sorry." T.J. sat on the bed in Amos's room. "I only pulled Dunc into that secret passage so I could show you guys how easy it is to listen to someone's conversation without them knowing. I didn't know he would look through the eyes in the painting. We're going to have to be very careful."

"Yeah," Amos growled. "Careful about which cousins we trust in the future."

"How did you find that passage?" Dunc asked.

"I guess you could say I fell into it. I was testing my latest invention. I think I told you about it in one of my letters—antigravity air shoes? Anyway, they got away from me on the stairs, and I grabbed that ugly little stone statue to keep from falling. When I pulled on it, the wall just sort of opened up—and there it was."

"Have you explored the whole passage?"

"No. Only parts of it. I'm pretty sure it goes all over the lower part of the castle. But I've only been to the kitchen and the library."

"Then how do you know it's safe for us to talk in here?" Dunc looked around Amos's room. A sword and shield hung on one wall and a tapestry on another. The only furniture was a four-poster bed, a nightstand, a dresser, and an overstuffed chair. A large stone fireplace was built into the corner.

"I don't. So far I haven't found any way they could listen up here, but that doesn't mean—"

"Wait a minute." Amos held up his hand.

"Headless ghosts, secret passages. Who's listening? What's going on here?"

"That's what you guys are going to help me find out. I hope." T.J. lowered his voice. "At night you can hear these strange sounds. And everybody around here acts like they're hiding something."

"That's it?" Amos shook his head. "That's all you've got? You dragged us halfway around the world and made me miss my date with Melissa to tell us that you've been hearing things?"

"You'll see for yourself, later tonight," T.J. said. "So you finally got a date with Melissa?"

"I was about to. See, she called to invite me to this dance, but I didn't quite make it to the phone."

"If you never made it to the phone, how do you know Melissa was calling you?"

"Don't confuse him with reality," Dunc said. "What does your dad think about all this?"

T.J. sighed. "Dad says he can't hear anything from his room. He thinks it's probably a case of too much rich Scottish food just before bedtime."

"Speaking of food"—Amos picked up his candle—"which way to the kitchen?"

"Go on down, Amos," Dunc said. "We'll be right behind you."

Amos took a step toward the door. He stopped. Dead. "Why don't we all go down together? Close together."

"Hold on." T.J. jumped off the bed. "I just remembered, I have something else to show you. Wait here. I'll be right back."

Dunc pulled a notepad from his pocket and moved closer to Amos's candle and started writing.

Amos's shoulders drooped. "Don't do that."

"What?"

"Don't start with that notebook stuff. When you do that, it means you're about to play private eye."

"A good detective always takes notes. I've explained this to you before. Someday when we're famous, you'll be thanking me."

"I'm sure."

T.J. came back into the room carrying a bottle. "I found this in the secret passage."

Dunc took the bottle. "There's no label. What is it?"

T.J. popped the lid off. "Take a whiff."

"Uggh!"

"What is it?" Amos asked. "Poison?"

"Worse." Dunc put the lid back on. "I think it's—whisky."

# Chapter · 5

The headless suit of armor made loud clanking noises as it floated through the air. It was coming right at him. Amos rolled to the side just as it reached for him.

Amos landed on the stone floor beside his bed. He opened his eyes, sat up, and looked around the room. No ghosts. No suit of armor. It was a dream. He let out a sigh of relief and shook his head. "Dunc told me I'd have nightmares if I ate that fifth piece of apple pie."

He sat in the dark for a few minutes wondering where he had left his candle. Then he heard the loud clanking noise again.

It wasn't a dream. He felt around on the night table for matches. Three tries, and he finally managed to light his candle. He searched the room. Nothing.

Amos sat down on the bed. "This is crazy. It's probably the high altitude. I'm not getting enough oxygen to my brain."

He started to blow out the candle when he heard it again: a loud noise like metal hitting metal. It seemed to be coming from inside the fireplace.

Amos cautiously inched over to the fireplace. He stepped up onto the hearth and looked in. Nothing unusual—just a regular everyday fireplace. Amos turned to step back down. His bare foot landed on something sharp. He jerked it up and fell backward against the wall of the fireplace. It started to move.

Amos screamed, just before being swallowed by the fireplace.

"Amos?" Dunc, hearing the scream, came flying into Amos's room. T.J. was on his heels. Dunc pointed his pen flashlight at the bed. "He's gone."

T.J. held his candle up. "Listen. I hear something."

"It's coming from over there." Dunc threw the light on the fireplace. "Amos?"

"I'm in here." The voice was muffled, blurred.

"Amos, what are you doing behind the fireplace?"

"Checking for termites. Don't be stupid. Get me out of here!"

"How'd you get back there? I can't find a door."

"There's no door. I fell on this lever, and the whole wall turned around."

T.J. stepped close to the back of the fireplace. "Amos, push on the lever again."

"I can't find it. My candle went out. I dropped it when the wall turned."

Dunc searched the wall. He pushed and pulled on everything. "There's nothing on this side."

"I've got an idea." T.J. headed for the door. "Tell Amos to hang on. The cavalry's coming."

"What's going on out there?" Amos yelled through the wall. "Are you guys going to get me out of here or what?"

"T.J.'s working on something."

"Tell him to hurry. There are big hairy creatures keeping me company back here."

Dunc could hear muffled voices coming from behind the wall. "Amos? Are you okay?"

The wall slowly creaked open.

Amos blasted through the opening. T.J. followed carrying a small white mouse. "Here's his big hairy creature."

Amos shrugged. "It was dark."

Dunc looked at T.J. "How'd you get back there?"

T.J. put the mouse on the floor. "I figured if his fireplace did it, mine would too. I was right."

"This is great." Dunc sat on the arm of the overstuffed chair. "There are probably secret passages all over this place. Tomorrow we'll follow as many as we can, and—"

"Not this boy." Amos shook his head. "Huh-uh."

"Why not?" Dunc asked. "Don't you want to find out what's going on here?"

"I already know something weird is going on. That's why I'm not going."

T.J. looked puzzled. "I don't get it. Earlier, you said you thought—"

"That was earlier. Before I heard the—it."

"You heard the noise?" T.J. asked. "What did it sound like to you?"

"It sounded like a machine—that walks—

and has big yellow monster eyes—and eats people."

"Amos." Dunc gave him a look.

Amos hated it when Dunc said his name like that. As if he were a three-year-old. "Well, it did."

"That's what I thought too," T.J. said. "I mean, I thought it sounded like some kind of machine."

Dunc rubbed his chin. "I wonder why anyone would go to the trouble to hide a machine in an old Scottish castle."

# Chapter · 6

"Aren't you dressed yet?" T.J. poked his head in Amos's room. "Mrs. Knox has breakfast ready."

"If you recall, I didn't get much sleep last night." Amos tied his shoe. "Something to do with fake fireplaces, loud noises, secret passages . . ."

"Well, try to hurry. We've got major investigating to do today."

"You've been hanging around Dunc too long. You're starting to sound like him."

"Thanks."

"It wasn't a compliment."

T.J. took the stairs two at a time. Amos

**29**

slumped down them still half-asleep. Dunc was already in the kitchen eating.

Amos sat down at the end of a long wooden table. In front of him was a bowl of something white and runny. "What's this stuff?"

"Porridge, young man. And all you'll be gettin', so eat up."

Amos looked up and found himself staring into the black eyes of an old woman with scraggly gray hair. Her back was bent, and her nose was long and crooked. The only thing missing was a wart on her nose.

"Amos, this is Mrs. Knox," T.J. said. "Mrs. Knox, my cousin Amos Binder."

She studied him for a long time. Amos hoped she wasn't considering turning him into a frog.

"Eat."

"Yes, ma'am." Amos nervously picked up his spoon. He looked at the stuff in the bowl. It reminded him of the snot that Jimmy Farrell always had dripping off the end of his nose. He put some of it in his mouth. It really wasn't too bad, if he pretended he was back home eating Fruit Slams. And if he didn't think about Jimmy Farrell.

Mrs. Knox sat down at the table with a cup

**30**

of tea. She drank it in one noisy gulp and then concentrated on the leaves in the bottom. She started talking out loud in a high-pitched voice to no one in particular. "I see three grasshoppers. Hopping here, hopping there. They're having such a lark—but then they hop somewhere they shouldn't be and see things they shouldn't see—and then all three get mashed. Flatter than an English pancake."

The last line tickled her. She started cackling like a hen laying an egg.

"Thanks for breakfast, Mrs. Knox." T.J. pushed his bowl away and stood up. "We've got a lot of sight-seeing to do today, so I guess we'd better get started. Oh, and don't worry about lunch. We'll take care of it ourselves."

Dunc and Amos followed him out the door.

Mrs. Knox screeched after them, "We're having haggis for supper. Don't be late."

Amos leaned up to T.J.'s ear. "Who's Haggis?"

"It's not a who. It's a what. Haggis is a famous Scottish dish made from the organs of a sheep—heart, liver, and lungs. They boil them in a bag made from the sheep's stomach."

Amos made a face. "Couldn't we just order out for pizza?"

T.J. grinned. "Don't worry, I've got a stash of candy bars in my room. And we can always go down to the village for a quick meal."

"There's a village near here?" Dunc asked.

"Sure. Dunbar Village. It's a fishing village right on the coast. I go there all the time when I'm not working in my laboratory."

"You have your own laboratory?" Amos was impressed. "Can we see it?"

T.J. blushed. "Well, I guess it's not a real laboratory. Dad gave me a room to work on my inventions. I finally got the bugs worked out of my magnetic signal retriever. But I'm still having problems with those air shoes."

Amos patted him on the back. "Don't worry, T.J., you'll get it. Genius runs in our family."

Dunc rolled his eyes. "I hate to break this up, but we have a case to solve."

"Right," T.J. said. "And like my grandmother always says, 'The early bird scratches the bald spot on the top of your head.'"

Dunc looked at T.J. He thought about asking him to explain that one but decided it would be smarter to let it drop. "Let's walk down to the village. I have a feeling we need to check it out if we're going to get anywhere on this case."

# Chapter·7

Amos opened the front door. He took two steps and ran face-first into a man's chest. A man wearing a tweed jacket and a red plaid skirt.

The man looked down his nose at him. "Excuse me, young man. I'm Mr. Macbeth, the realtor for this property. I was just about to knock."

T.J. pulled Amos back. "These are my friends from America, Mr. Macbeth. This is—"

The man curled his upper lip. "Yes, I heard you had some little friends staying with you. Is your father in?"

"My dad's at work. Can I help you?"

35

"I need to check on some things for the owner of the property. If you don't mind, I'd like to speak to the housekeeper."

"She's in the kitchen." T.J. moved so that the man could get past.

Mr. Macbeth walked through the front door and headed for the kitchen without a backward glance at the boys.

"Hmmm." Dunc tapped his chin. "There's something strange about that guy."

Amos shrugged. "He seemed okay to me— if you don't count the dress."

"That was a kilt." Dunc continued to tap his chin. "In Scotland men sometimes wear kilts to signify which clan they belong to."

"If it's not the dress, then what's bothering you?" Amos asked.

"Well, for starters, how did he know T.J. had friends staying with him?"

"Dad and I didn't tell him," T.J. said. "We didn't even know ourselves for sure until yesterday."

"And if he really came to see your dad, why didn't he come in the afternoon, when he'd be sure and catch him at home?"

"Is he a suspect?" T.J. asked.

Dunc nodded. "It looks that way."

"Couldn't we talk about this on the way to town?" Amos asked. "I'm starving."

"We'll go in a minute. Right now, we've got more important things to do." Dunc took his pen flashlight out and flashed it on and off to make sure it was still working.

Amos frowned. "What could be more important than eating?"

Dunc looked at T.J. "Didn't you say the passage from the staircase leads to the kitchen?"

T.J. nodded. "And who knows where else. I haven't explored all of it."

"Come on." Dunc led the way to the stairs. He pulled on the statue, and the secret door slid open. "Let's find out what our friend Mr. Macbeth is up to."

Amos stopped. "Wait a minute. What about that monster we heard last night? He's probably running loose in there somewhere, looking for his next victim. Maybe I should stay out here and keep watch."

"You can't stay out here," Dunc said. "Somebody might see you and wonder where T.J. and I are."

"I'll tell them you're in the bathroom."

"Both of us?"

Amos shrugged. "When you gotta go . . ."

"Someone's coming," T.J. whispered.

Dunc pulled Amos inside the passage and shut the door. He fumbled for his pen flashlight. "Which way to the kitchen?"

T.J. led them to the right, down a narrow, musky-smelling tunnel. They followed him in silence until they reached a dead end. Voices were coming from the other side of the wall.

Amos started to say something, but Dunc put his finger to his lips.

Mrs. Knox sounded angry. She was practically yelling. "You said it would just be the professor! Then he shows up with his brat. And if that ain't enough, two more whelps from America show up. Before long, they'll have a regular dog-and-pony show."

Mr. Macbeth's voice was calm. "They're just kids. What can they hurt?"

"If they find out, they can hurt plenty. My boy Jimmy don't like it. He's thinking of getting out while there's still time."

"Don't be ridiculous. You can tell Jimmy and the others that everything is under control. We wanted a good cover for our operation, didn't we? Well, now we have it. Those Yanks don't have a clue."

# Chapter · 8

Dunc checked the stairs. "It's all clear. Come on."

Dunc and T.J. bounded down the stairs and out the front door. Amos would have followed except for one small problem: The back of his jacket was caught in the secret door.

Mrs. Knox moved into the great hall and started dusting the furniture. She noticed Amos on the stairs. "You up there. What are you doing?"

Amos looked around. "Me?"

Mrs. Knox put her hands on her hips. "I don't see no one else up there."

Amos gulped. "I'm not doing anything. Just hanging around."

"Well, do it somewhere else. I've got work to do in here."

The front door opened, and Dunc stood in the opening. The door blocked Dunc's view of Mrs. Knox, who was dusting an antique bookshelf. He looked up at Amos. "Aren't you coming?"

"Nope."

"What?"

"You heard me. I said I'm not coming."

"Why not?"

Amos tried to point to Mrs. Knox with his head. "I like it up here. There's an outstanding view of the . . . wall from here. I may stand here all afternoon."

"Don't be dumb—what's wrong with your head?"

Amos let out an exasperated sigh. "Maybe you and T.J. should go on to town without me. I'll just stay here and enjoy the view." He rolled his eyes in Mrs. Knox's direction.

T.J. pushed by Dunc. "What's the holdup?"

Dunc shrugged. "Amos wants to stay here."

Mrs. Knox picked up her dusting supplies and stormed off into the kitchen. "A body can't get no work done around here with all this commotion."

T.J. looked up at Amos. "Want us to bring you anything from town?"

"Get up here!"

Dunc scratched his head. "But I thought you said—"

"I'll give you two seconds to get up here. Then I'm going to wiggle out of this coat and strangle both of you."

"Why didn't you tell me you were stuck?" Dunc pulled on the statue.

Amos jerked his coat out of the crack. "All this time I thought you two were so smart." He stomped down the stairs. "My dog Scruff has more brains in his little toe." He headed out the door mumbling to himself. "My goldfish could out-think both of you put together. A rock has more intelligence. . . ."

"What's wrong with him?" T.J. asked.

"Who knows. Sometimes he gets like this. Don't worry. It never lasts long."

Amos was almost to the bridge when they caught up with him.

# Chapter·9

"You call this a town? There's not even a traffic light! Where's the mall? The arcade?"

"It's a fishing village, Amos," T.J. said. "About all they have are a few shops, a couple of pubs, and a fish market."

Amos sniffed the air and nudged Dunc. "Does this place remind you of anything?"

Dunc crinkled his nose. "The waterfront back home. I hope the people are nicer."

"Tell me again why we're here?"

"We're looking for clues. Anything that might tell us what's going on up at the castle."

"Do we have to look for clues on an empty stomach?" Amos asked.

"There's a place across the street that

makes pretty good food." T.J. pointed at a sign that said "Macdonald's." "The menu is sort of limited, though."

"Are you kidding?" Amos snorted. "We have those at home. I eat there all the time."

"But Amos, it's not—"

Amos wasn't listening. He crossed the street and looked inside the door. The room was dark, and there were several steps leading down to the main floor. One side of the room was a bar. The other side had a few empty tables.

Amos took a step back. He looked at T.J. "Are you sure this is the right place?"

"I'm sure." T.J. led them to a table. "This is definitely Macdonald's. Rosie Macdonald's."

When they were seated, a woman wearing a white cup towel for an apron came over to their table. "What'll it be, gents?"

Amos cleared his throat. "I'll have a double cheeseburger, fries, a large chocolate shake, and—"

The woman grinned. "That'll be one order of fish and chips." She rolled the r's in the word *order*. "How about you two?"

"We'll have the same." T.J. turned to Amos. "I told you the menu was limited."

Dunc leaned over the table. "Don't look now, but I think we've been followed."

T.J. and Amos turned around. Mr. Smith, the grounds keeper from the castle, was coming down the steps.

"I said don't look."

"I knew he'd turn up," T.J. said. "He's everywhere. I haven't been able to make a move without him following me."

Mr. Smith walked over to the bar. He whispered something to Rosie and handed her a piece of paper. Without looking around, he turned and left the building.

"That was strange," T.J. said. "Usually he stays right with me."

Dunc watched Rosie working behind the counter. "I wonder what was on that piece of paper."

"That's not hard to figure," Amos said. "He placed an order to go."

Dunc shook his head. "He didn't wait for any food."

"Oh, yeah."

"She's probably an international spy," T.J. whispered. "And he gave her a coded message."

Amos put his elbow on the table. "You've

**45**

been watching too many old James Bond movies."

T.J. looked offended. "I've learned a lot from James Bond." He took a pen out of the inside pocket of his trench coat. "Take this, for example."

Amos reached for it. "What does it do? Write in disappearing ink?"

"Among other things." T.J. jerked it out of his reach. "Watch this." He touched a button, and a tiny pair of scissors slid up out of the handle.

"That's handy," Amos said, "if you want to cut out paper dolls or something."

T.J. stuck his bottom lip out. "Okay, you asked for it." He pointed the pen at Amos and pushed another button. Nothing happened. "It must be stuck. It's supposed to squirt ink in your face. I guess I'll have to work on it."

He banged it on the table just as Rosie brought their food. A big ink blob splattered her apron.

T.J. jumped up, dipped his napkin in his glass of water, and tried to wipe it off, but he only succeeded in smearing it. "I'm terribly sorry, Mrs. Macdonald. I was just showing my friends how my pen worked, and—"

**46**

"Sit down quickly, boy. You're drawing attention to us." She set the food on the table. Then she laid the ticket upside down beside Dunc. "Be sure you check that ticket carefully, boy. You never know. It might surprise you."

Dunc waited until she was on her way back to the counter, then picked up the ticket. Only it wasn't a ticket. It was a piece of paper with a message on it.

Keep your noses where they belong. There's trouble in the offing.

P.S. Stay in your rooms at night.

Amos frowned. "It doesn't make sense. What language is it written in?"

Dunc stuffed the paper into his pocket. "That's the way these guys talk over here. I think Mr. Smith's trying to warn us about something. Hurry and finish eating. We need to go someplace where we can talk."

# Chapter · 10

Dunc stopped on the old bridge in front of the castle and took out his notebook. "Let's see. So far we have: a weird noise we can't explain, a bottle of whisky, a suspicious conversation involving the housekeeper and Mr. Macbeth, and a strange message from Mr. Smith. Have I left out anything?"

"Yeah," Amos said. "The monster."

Dunc shook his head. "We haven't determined that there is a monster."

Amos sighed. "The problem is, we haven't determined there isn't. It's all in how you look at it."

Dunc flipped the notebook shut. "This is

**49**

one of the most puzzling cases I've ever had. Nothing fits."

Amos leaned over the side of the bridge and threw a rock into the stream. "I vote we forget it and go fishing."

T.J. opened his trench coat. "Your wish is my command." He reached deep into a side pocket and produced a short pole and a miniature tackle box.

"I take back what I said earlier. You're amazing, T.J." Amos took the pole and headed for the water.

"Not really. My dad told me there was trout fishing up here, so I came prepared."

Amos followed a trail that led underneath the old bridge. He put the pole together and baited his hook. "Come on down here, you guys. Watch the master fisherman at work."

Dunc and T.J. worked their way down the steep trail. Dunc sat down in the shade of the bridge. "The last time I watched the master fisherman, he got his line caught in someone else's lunch basket. He wound up catching the biggest bologna sandwich on the dock."

"That was back when I was an amateur. I'm better now. I've been practicing."

"I didn't know you'd been down to the

dock," Dunc said. "You didn't say anything about it."

"I don't tell you everything. Besides, I wasn't practicing at the dock."

"If it wasn't at the dock, then where—"

Amos cast out into the stream. "There's this new program on channel nine. It comes on every afternoon before my mom gets home from work. It's all about different kinds of fishing techniques."

"So where have you been practicing?" Dunc asked.

Amos reeled in. "I've always been one of those hands-on type learners. You know, actually do the thing while the teacher's explaining it."

"I have a feeling he's trying to tell us he practices in his living room," T.J. said.

"Oh." Dunc watched him cast. "What do your parents think of that?"

"I don't think it would have been that big of a problem if my mom hadn't come home early with her Welcome Wagon group."

"What happened?" Dunc asked.

"The show that day was on fly fishing. I made a spectacular cast just as Mrs. Higgins, the mayor's wife, walked in our front door.

The hook landed on her head. I knew if I didn't handle it just right, I'd be in trouble. So I gave it a gentle pull and reeled my line back in. The only problem was, her hair came with it. How was I supposed to know Mrs. Higgins was bald?"

T.J. laughed. "Then what happened?"

"Mrs. Higgins wasn't a very good sport about it. She busted my new pole over my head and stomped out the door. My mother threw out all my fishing gear and said if I ever touched a fishing pole again, *I'd* be bald."

Dunc was about to remind Amos that he had his hands on a fishing pole when he heard someone talking on the bridge overhead.

"I'll be glad when we get this shipment ready. Things are getting too dangerous with those kids hanging around. The boss says we can lay low awhile after we get this one out."

"I don't think it's the kids you're worried about, Jimmy Knox. I think it's himself. The ghost of Robert Ramsey. Your mother has you scared to death at the mention of his name."

The two men walked on over the bridge and out of hearing range. Amos recognized the look on Dunc's face. That look meant trouble.

# Chapter · 11

They were in T.J.'s laboratory. Dunc and T.J. were hovered over a desk making plans. Amos was playing with a remote-control flyswatter.

Dunc looked up. "Pay attention, Amos. You're not going to know what's going on."

"I don't want to know what's going on. That way I don't have to be a part of it."

T.J. held up a drawing. "Look at this, Amos. It's a drawing of our secret weapon."

"I don't need to look. I know it's not going to work."

"What makes you so sure?" T.J. asked.

"Two reasons. First, the odds are bad. Dunc's never had a plan yet that actually worked. And second, nobody in their right mind would wander up and down dark secret passages at night with a vicious, people-eating monster running loose."

Dunc frowned. "How many times do I have to tell you? There's no monster. Besides, we need you for this."

"As what—bait?"

"Of course not. You have the key role."

Amos eyed them both suspiciously. "Just what exactly do you have in mind?"

T.J. brought the drawing over. "See, we have this costume—"

Amos took the paper. "That looks like the suit of armor on the stairs."

Dunc nodded. "It is."

"Are you both crazy? You want me to wear a suit of armor? It's too heavy. I won't be able to move."

"Isn't it great, Amos?" T.J. added some detail to the drawing. "Dunc thought of it. He got the idea when Jimmy Knox said he was afraid of the headless ghost, Robert Ramsey."

"Why do I get stuck with the armor? Why don't one of you boy geniuses wear it?"

"We thought of that," T.J. said. "But you're

the tallest, so it will fit you better, and Dunc and I have other things to do."

"Like what?"

T.J. picked up something off the table. "Like making sure these antigravity air shoes have enough power to hold you and the suit of armor up in the air. You have to look like you're floating."

Amos took one of the shoes and looked it over. "I thought you said you didn't have all the bugs worked out of these yet."

T.J. grabbed the shoe. "I will have—by tonight."

Dunc brought a chair over. "Sit down, Amos. Let me explain the plan."

Amos slumped down in the chair. "If it's the usual, I kill myself while looking like a total idiot and you two come out without a scratch."

# **Chapter·12**

"Come on, Amos, it's getting late." Dunc pulled him up off the bed. "You have to practice walking. We want to be ready when we hear the noise."

Amos tapped on the outside of his armor. "I feel like the tin man in *The Wizard of Oz*." He peeked up over the top of the neckpiece. "I can barely see where I'm going."

"Let's try the shoes," T.J. said. "You activate them by tapping the heels together—"

"Like I said, *The Wizard of Oz*."

"—and you deactivate them by pulling on the shoestrings. Try it."

"Shhh." Dunc put his finger to his lips. "Did you hear that?"

A muffled clanking sound came from behind the fireplace.

"That's it," Dunc said. "They're back there somewhere. Now's our chance to find out what's going on."

"But Dunc"—T.J. frowned—"we haven't had a chance to test it yet. What if it doesn't work?"

"It'll work." Dunc led Amos to the fireplace. "Trust me."

Amos snorted. "You could have gone all night without saying that."

T.J. grabbed some extra candles and moved inside the fireplace. "Ready or not, here we come." He pulled the lever and the wall slowly turned around.

Dunc flipped on his flashlight. "It sounds like it's coming from that direction." He started off down the dark tunnel.

"Wait for me," Amos whispered. "I'm carrying a few extra pounds here."

Dunc trotted back. "Put your arms around us. We'll help carry some of the weight until we get close."

T.J. wiggled underneath one of Amos's arms. "Isn't this exciting?"

"That's not what I would call it," Amos said. "Stupid is more—"

Dunc stopped. "We're getting closer. The noise is louder. You guys wait here. I'm going up ahead to check things out."

They waited in the dark for a few minutes. T.J. lit one of his candles. "I wonder what's taking him so long? Maybe I better make sure he's okay."

Amos grabbed T.J.'s arm. "He said to wait."

"Here." T.J. lit another candle and handed it to him. "I'll be right back."

Amos thought about sitting down, but he couldn't figure out how. He leaned up against the wall and waited. And waited.

"Dunc? T.J.? You guys aren't playing tricks on me again, are you?" Amos moved slowly down the passage the way they had gone. A man's hand reached silently from the cover of a side tunnel. It hit the armor and glanced off. Amos didn't feel it. He kept moving toward the noise at the end of the passage.

He rounded the next corner and stopped. The passage opened up into a large room set up like a factory. One man was putting empty bottles into a machine, and another man was slapping labels on them as fast as they came out.

Amos took a step back and accidentally rubbed his heels together. He could feel himself slowly rising off the floor. He frantically reached for his shoelaces but the armor wouldn't let him bend.

The ceiling was coming closer. Amos ducked through the archway into the factory. He tried walking in backward in the air, but every time he moved, he lunged forward.

The men in the room stopped working and stared at him. For a minute he had them worried. He floated across the room like a ghost with no head. It might have worked the way Dunc said it would—if one of his shoelaces hadn't gotten caught on the corner of a machine.

One air shoe deactivated immediately. The heavy armor started to tilt sideways. Amos could feel his top half losing altitude. He was hanging upside down. One leg was suspended straight up, the other pedaling frantically trying to get upright. Amos reached up for his other shoelace. He managed to grab the tip and pull.

His landing could have been better.

A couple of inches to the left, and he would have missed the large vat of homemade whisky. As it was, he hit it dead center. He might have drowned if two of the workers hadn't pulled him out.

Jimmy Knox sneered at him. "It's one of them snoopy kids. Tie him up until the boss figures out what to do with him."

"I think not." Mr. Smith was standing in the doorway with several policemen. "Put your hands in the air."

# Chapter · 13

Mr. Smith lit his pipe. "Scotland Yard has had this place under surveillance for several months. We had reports of bootlegging in this area but no solid evidence."

Dunc sat on the sofa in the great room. "You mean these guys were running an illegal whisky-making operation?"

Mr. Smith nodded. "Mr. Macbeth was the brains behind it. It was his idea to rent the castle to you as a cover for the operation. He hired Mrs. Knox and her son and a few others to make sure things went smoothly. When I grabbed you boys in the tunnel, we were just about to make our arrest."

"How about you?" T.J. asked. "Who hired you?"

"I was hired by the owner. When I showed my letter of employment to Mr. Macbeth, he had no choice but to accept it."

"Who is the owner?" T.J.'s dad asked.

Mr. Smith cleared his throat. "The Queen."

T.J.'s eyes popped wide open. "You work for the Queen?"

"I do. And I have been in touch with Her Majesty this very morning, and she wishes me to convey her appreciation to you boys for your help in providing—shall we say—the little distraction that allowed us to get the edge on our suspects."

T.J. turned to his father. "You should have seen my invention, Dad. Amos went clear to the ceiling. Hey—where is Amos anyway?"

Mr. Smith smiled. "Your friend and myself had a long conversation over breakfast about—"

An ear-splitting noise came from the top of the stairs. Amos was standing on the landing blowing into a set of bagpipes. He was dressed in a red plaid kilt.

Amos took a breath. "What do you guys think?" He turned all the way around to give the full effect. "Mr. Smith says this getup really impresses the girls over here. I thought I'd try it on Melissa."

Complete silence.

"What?" Amos looked down at himself. "Is it the dress? Too much knee? What?"

Mr. Tyler and Mr. Smith headed for the kitchen. T.J. and Dunc were moving fast toward the front door.

"Where's everybody going? Don't you want to hear my next song?"

The front door slammed.

Amos stared after them, wondering what was wrong. He shrugged, and a happy look crawled across his face.

Maybe, he thought, I should call Melissa and play a song for her. That's it. A sneak preview of coming attractions. She'll probably meet me at the airport. The music will win her over. I'll have to fight her off. But I won't be pushy, play it slow. I'll wait a couple of days to announce our engagement. . . .

**Be sure to join Dunc and Amos in these other Culpepper Adventures:**

### *The Case of the Dirty Bird*

When Dunc Culpepper and his best friend, Amos, first see the parrot in a pet store, they're not impressed—it's smelly, scruffy, and missing half its feathers. They're only slightly impressed when they learn that the parrot speaks four languages, has outlived ten of its owners, and is probably 150 years old. But when the bird starts mouthing off about buried treasure, Dunc and Amos get pretty excited—let the amateur sleuthing begin!

### *Dunc's Doll*

Dunc and his accident-prone friend Amos are up to their old sleuthing habits once again. This time they're after a band of doll thieves! When a doll that once belonged to Charles Dickens's daughter is stolen from an exhibition at the local mall, the two boys put on their detective gear and do some serious snooping. Will a vicious watchdog keep them from retrieving the valuable missing doll?

## Culpepper's Cannon

Dunc and Amos are researching the Civil War cannon that stands in the town square when they find a note inside telling them about a time portal. Entering it through the dressing room of La Petite, a women's clothing store, the boys find themselves in downtown Chatham on March 8, 1862—the day before the historic clash between the *Monitor* and the *Merrimac*. But the Confederate soldiers they meet mistake them for Yankee spies. Will they make it back to the future in one piece?

## Dunc Gets Tweaked

Dunc and Amos meet up with a new buddy named Lash when they enter the radical world of skateboard competition. When somebody "cops"— steals—Lash's prototype skateboard, the boys are determined to get it back. After all, Lash is about to shoot for a totally rad world's record! Along the way they learn a major lesson: *Never* kiss a monkey!

## Dunc's Halloween

Dunc and Amos are planning the best route to get the most candy on Halloween. But their plans change when Amos is slightly bitten by a werewolf. He begins scratching himself and chasing UPS trucks: he's become a werepuppy!

### Dunc Breaks the Record

Dunc and Amos have a small problem when they try hang gliding—they crash in the wilderness. Luckily, Amos has read a book about a boy who survived in the wilderness for fifty-four days. Too bad Amos doesn't have a hatchet. Things go from bad to worse when a wild man holds the boys captive. Can anything save them now?

### Dunc and the Flaming Ghost

Dunc's not afraid of ghosts, although Amos is sure that the old Rambridge house is haunted by the ghost of Blackbeard the Pirate. Then the best friends meet Eddie, a meek man who claims to be impersonating Blackbeard's ghost in order to live in the house in peace. But if that's true, why are flames shooting from his mouth?

### Amos Gets Famous

Deciphering a code they find in a library book, Amos and Dunc stumble onto a burglary ring. The burglars' next target is the home of Melissa, the girl of Amos's dreams (who doesn't even know that he's alive). Amos longs to be a hero to Melissa, so nothing will stop him from solving this case—not even a mind-boggling collision with a jock, a chimpanzee, and a toilet.

### Dunc and Amos Hit the Big Top

In order to impress Melissa, Amos decides to perform on the trapeze at the visiting circus. Look out below! But before Dunc can talk him out of his plan, the two stumble across a mystery behind the scenes at the circus. Now Amos is in double trouble. What's really going on under the big top?

### Dunc's Dump

Camouflaged as piles of rotting trash, Dunc and Amos are sneaking around the town dump. Dunc wants to find out who is polluting the garbage at the dump with hazardous and toxic waste. Amos just wants to impress Melissa. Can either of them succeed?

### Dunc and the Scam Artists

Dunc and Amos are at it again. Some older residents of their town have been bilked by con artists, and the two boys want to look into these crimes. They meet elderly Betsy Dell, whose nasty nephew Frank gives the boys the creeps. Then they notice some soft dirt in Ms. Dell's shed, and a shovel. Does Frank have something horrible in store for Dunc and Amos?

### Dunc and Amos and the Red Tattoos

Dunc and Amos head for camp and face two weeks of fresh air—along with regulations, demerits, K.P., and inedible food. But where these two best friends go, trouble follows. They overhear a threat against the camp director and discover that camp funds have been stolen. Do these crimes have anything to do with the tattoo of the exotic red flower that some of the camp staff have on their arms?

### Dunc's Undercover Christmas

It's Christmastime! and Dunc, Amos, and Amos's cousin T.J. hit the mall for some serious shopping. But when the seasonal magic is threatened by some disappearing presents and Santa Claus himself is a prime suspect, the boys put their celebration on hold and go undercover in perfect Christmas disguises! Can the sleuthing trio protect Santa's threatened reputation and catch the impostor before he strikes again?

## *The Wild Culpepper Cruise*

When Amos wins a "Why I Love My Dog" contest, he and Dunc are off on the Caribbean cruise of their dreams! But there's something downright fishy about Amos's suitcase, and before they know it, the two best friends wind up with more high seas adventure than they bargained for. Can Dunc and Amos figure out who's out to get them and salvage what's left of their vacation?